The Final Battle

The Final Battle

A. L. Singer

LUCAS BOOKS

SCHOLASTIC INC.

New York • Toronto • London • Auckland • Sydney
Mexico City • New Delhi • Hong Kong • Buenos Aires

ISBN 0-439-45892-7

12 11 10 9 8 7 6 5 4 3 2   3 4 5 6 7 8/0

Printed in the U.S.A.
First Scholastic printing, November 2000

The Final Battle

CHAPTER ONE

Everything was in a name, Qui-Gon thought.

Sith.

The sound itself was poisonous. A snake's hiss, a gas leak, a lightsaber's deadly arc.

A whisper. A secret.

The attacker on the planet Tatooine had fought with the skill and savagery that could only belong to a Sith. The Force was dark around him. There was only one problem: The Sith didn't exist.

Qui-Gon Jinn knew about them the way he knew about the great Jedi battles—as ancient history. As the reminder of a barbaric time when the Galactic Republic was young and the forces of darkness rampant.

The Sith were a band of Jedi Knights, fallen to the ways of the dark side. Harnessing the dark side of the Force, they had threatened to take over the Republic, but they were driven away by the Jedi Knights. During the time that followed, a prosperous golden age, the Sith had faded into legend.

But the man with the red and black tattooed face was no mythic character. He was flesh and bone, reflex and power.

Had the Sith lain dormant for eons, recruiting warriors and rebuilding strength? If so, what were they doing on Tatooine? And why had one of them attacked Qui-Gon?

Qui-Gon had been on Tatooine for ship repairs on his way to the planet Coruscant, where he was to deliver Queen Amidala of Naboo. There, before the

Senate, the Queen was to plead for support against the Trade Federation's attack on her people.

Qui-Gon's conclusion—that the Trade Federation was aligned with a surviving band of Sith—seemed incredible. He vowed to bring the matter before the Jedi High Council at their headquarters on Coruscant— along with another important request.

Now that his Padawan learner, Obi-Wan Kenobi, was ready to become a Jedi Knight, Qui-Gon wanted to champion a new apprentice. Anakin Skywalker was the most extraordinary Jedi candidate he had ever seen, perhaps even the Chosen One.

The boy and his mother, both slaves for a parts dealer named Watto, had befriended Qui-Gon on Tatooine. Qui-Gon, with no Tatooine money, could not get the hyperdrive he needed from Watto—until he made a bet. He wagered the hyperdrive on a victory by Anakin in the annual Boonta Eve Podrace—against the toughest competition in the galaxy—and the boy did it. Before the win, Qui-Gon had tested Anakin's blood. The amount of the boy's midi-chlorians, the embodiment of the Force in all beings, was astronomical.

Obi-Wan disapproved of recruiting a boy at his age. Anakin was nine years old, far too old to begin such training. According to Jedi wisdom, after the age of three, the forces of fear and darkness were already too deeply implanted in a child. But, Qui-Gon had a feeling about this boy. And Qui-Gon had learned to follow his feelings.

As the ship passed through the teeming vertical masses of Coruscant, the boy's face was pressed to the glass. Flying vehicles swarmed among the spires of skyscrapers that rose through clouds like steel stalagmites.

"Welcome to Coruscant, the capital of the Republic," said Ric Olié, the starship pilot. "The entire planet is one big city."

"Wow!" Anakin replied. "It's so huge!"

Obi-Wan smiled. All the boy had ever known was the desolate, sandy plains of Tatooine. From here on, everything in Anakin's life would be something of a shock.

* * *

Supreme Chancellor Valorum met the ship at the landing dock. He was a trim, stately man of great intellect. With him was Senator Palpatine of Naboo, renowned for his sharpness and political skill.

Qui-Gon descended the ramp with Obi-Wan and their amphibian Gungan companion, Jar Jar Binks. The three stepped aside and bowed as Queen Amidala emerged from the ship, followed by her handmaidens and Captain Panaka, head of Royal Security Forces on Naboo.

"It is a great gift to see you alive, Your Majesty,"

Senator Palpatine said. "May I present Supreme Chancellor Valorum."

"Welcome, Your Highness," Valorum said. "It is an honor to finally meet you in person. I must relay to you how distressed everyone is over the current situation. I've called for a special session of the Senate to hear your position."

"I am grateful for your concern, Chancellor," the Queen replied.

"There is a question of procedure," Senator Palpatine said, leading the Queen, her handmaidens, and Captain Panaka to a waiting air taxi, "but I feel confident that we can overcome it."

Queen Amidala gestured for Anakin and Jar Jar to follow.

Qui-Gon watched as they walked out of earshot. Then, he turned to the Supreme Chancellor and said softly, "I must speak with the Jedi Council immediately, Your Honor. The situation has become more complicated."

"As you wish," Valorum replied.

Immediately, he led Qui-Gon and Obi-Wan into a nearby transport, which sped toward the Jedi Temple.

"I was hoping you would stand with the Queen before the Senate," the Supreme Chancellor said.

"I'm afraid that your words will bear more weight than mine, Chancellor," Qui-Gon replied.

Valorum shook his head ruefully. "The Senate is chaotic these days. Someone has started a baseless rumor about me that has grown to a corruption scandal. It will be proven false, of course, but meanwhile my power has eroded. The bureaucrats are in charge—and while that is true, I'm afraid very little will be done about the Naboo issue."

Qui-Gon placed a reassuring hand on Valorum's shoulder. "The Queen's presence will change everything, you will see."

Soon, the Jedi Temple loomed before them. The transport docked, and Qui-Gon and Obi-Wan bade Valorum farewell.

They presented themselves at the gate, and an honor guard escorted them into the building.

As they approached the High Council chambers, Qui-Gon whispered to Obi-Wan, "Let me do the talking."

It was a large, round room with a high, panoramic view of the cityscape. The twelve Council members welcomed the two visitors warmly but cautiously. Qui-Gon had been before them several times—in some cases to be reprimanded for defying their edicts.

Qui-Gon knew he would have to tread lightly. This news was bound to surprise—even shock—them.

As the High Council members sat in their accustomed circle, Qui-Gon carefully described the warrior he had encountered on Tatooine. "My only conclusion," he said, "is that he was a Sith Lord."

Mace Windu, a senior member, was taken aback. "A Sith Lord?"

"Impossible!" exclaimed Ki-Adi-Mundi, the celebrated hero from the planet Cerea, whose curious high-domed forehead contained a second heart. "The Sith have been extinct for a millennium!"

Master Yoda nodded slowly. He was considered to be the wisest of all Jedi Masters, and although he disapproved of Qui-Gon's headstrong ways, Yoda had nevertheless taken a special interest in his career. "The very Republic is threatened," he said, "if involved the Sith are."

"I do not believe they could have returned without us knowing," Mace Windu said.

"Hard to see, the dark side is," Yoda replied. "Discover who this assassin is, we must."

"I sense he will reveal himself again," Ki-Adi suggested.

Mace Windu still seemed unconvinced. "This attack was with purpose, that is clear—and I agree that the Queen is his target..."

"With this Naboo queen you must stay, Qui-Gon," Yoda urged. "Protect her."

"We will use all our resources here to unravel this mystery and discover the identity of your attacker," Mace Windu vowed. "May the Force be with you."

"May the Force be with you," Yoda added.

Qui-Gon heard Obi-Wan beginning to leave, but he stood his ground. One more matter remained.

"Master Qui-Gon, more to say have you?" Yoda asked.

"With your permission, my Master, I have encountered a vergence in the Force."

Yoda's ears picked up. "A vergence, you say?"

"Located around a person?" Mace Windu asked.

"A boy. His cells have the highest concentration of midi-chlorians I have seen in a life-form." Qui-Gon paused, searching for words. "It is possible he was *conceived* by the midi-chlorians."

Mace Windu sat forward. "You're referring to the prophecy of the one who will bring balance to the Force. You believe it is this boy?"

"I don't presume—" Qui-Gon began to protest.

"But you do!" Yoda interrupted. "Revealed your opinion is."

"I request the boy be tested," Qui-Gon said.

The Council members communicated with one another through uncomfortable silent glances. Qui-Gon's heart sank. They didn't believe him.

"Trained as a Jedi, you request for him?" Yoda asked.

"Finding him was the will of the Force, I have no doubt of that," Qui-Gon pressed on. "There is too much happening here..."

"Bring him before us, then," said Mace Windu.

Yoda nodded. "Tested he will be."

CHAPTER TWO

Once outside the chamber, Obi-Wan broke his silence. "The boy will not pass the Council's tests, Master. He is far too old."

"Anakin *will* become a Jedi," Qui-Gon replied calmly. "I promise you."

"Don't defy the Council, Master. Not again."

"I will do what I must."

"Master, *you* could be sitting on the Council by now if you would just follow the code! They will not go along with you this time."

Qui-Gon smiled patiently. Obi-Wan was smart and strong—and with time, his mind would gain the flexibility to question rules. "You still have much to learn, my young apprentice...."

* * *

Anakin seemed eager about the testing, but also apprehensive. Qui-Gon did all he could to encourage him. The Council would soon see, Qui-Gon was convinced, that Anakin was more than worthy.

Now, as the boy faced the initial round of testing, Qui-Gon paced outside the High Council door. Through it, he heard snatches of the mind-reflex responses: As a Jedi Council Member held a holographic screen, Anakin, had to read what the Jedi was seeing.

"...a ship...a cup...a speeder..."

The boy's voice was steady, matter-of-fact. Qui-Gon could only hope he was accurate.

Obi-Wan leaned against a wall, eyeing his Master bemusedly.

Soon the voices inside grew louder. Mind-reflex was over and now came the grilling—putting Anakin under pressure, determining his readiness for a life of sacrifice and devotion, prodding him for mental weakness.

"I am not afraid!" Anakin's voice blurted out.

Qui-Gon cringed. The boy was angry, defensive. But Qui-Gon had been that way, too.

He could hear the lecture from Yoda: *Fear is the path to the dark side. Fear leads to anger. Anger leads to hate. Hate leads to suffering.*

Finally, the Council door was flung open. Master Yoda gestured for Qui-Gon and his Padawan to enter.

Anakin stood in the center of the circular floor. He managed a brave smile, but his face was drained.

"Correct you were, Qui-Gon," Yoda said softly.

Mace Windu nodded. "His cells contain a very high concentration of midi-chlorians."

"The Force is strong with him," Ki-Adi concurred.

"He's to be trained, then," Qui-Gon said hopefully.

Mace Windu shook his head. "No, he will not be trained."

"*No?*"

"He is too old. There is already too much anger in him."

For a moment, Qui-Gon was speechless.

The boy tried to contain his emotion. Obi-Wan, his own feelings now confirmed, tried to hold back a smile.

"He *is* the Chosen One," Qui-Gon insisted. "You must see it."

"Clouded this boy's future is," Yoda warned. "Masked by his youth."

"*I* will train him, then," Qui-Gon asserted. "I take Anakin as my Padawan learner."

"An apprentice you *have*, Qui-Gon," Yoda replied. "Impossible to take on a second."

Mace Windu nodded. "The code forbids it."

"Obi-Wan is ready—" Qui-Gon protested.

"I am ready to face the trials," Obi-Wan cut in.

"Ready so early, are you?" Yoda asked sharply. "What know you of ready?"

"He is headstrong, Master Yoda," Qui-Gon said, "and he has much to learn about the Living Force—but he is capable. There is little more he will learn from me."

"Our own counsel we will keep, on who is ready," Yoda shot back. "More to learn, he has."

"Now is not the time for this," Mace Windu said impatiently. "The Senate is voting for a new Supreme Chancellor. Queen Amidala is returning home, which will put pressure on the Trade Federation and could widen the confrontation."

"And draw out the Queen's attacker," Ki-Adi added. "Events are moving fast. Too fast."

"Qui-Gon, go with the Queen to Naboo and discover the identity of this dark warrior," Mace Windu instructed. "That is the clue we need to unravel this mystery of the Sith."

"Young Skywalker's fate will be decided later," Yoda declared.

Later. So there was a chance.

"I brought Anakin here—he must stay in my charge," Qui-Gon insisted. "He has nowhere else to go."

"He is your ward, Qui-Gon," Mace Windu concurred, "we will not dispute that."

"Train him not," Yoda commanded. "Take him with you, but train him not!"

"Protect the Queen," Mace Windu added, "but do not intercede if it comes to war, until we have the Senate's approval."

With a firm nod, Yoda indicated the end of the meeting. "May the Force be with you."

CHAPTER THREE

Anakin didn't speak a word to Qui-Gon and Obi-Wan during the ride back to the Senate. Upon arrival at the landing platform, he left the cab and walked listlessly among the vehicles. A stiff, cold wind tossed his hair. Even R2-D2's chirping presence didn't seem to cheer him up.

The landing platform was empty of people—clearly the Senate was still in session. Qui-Gon and his Padawan headed for the Naboo Royal Starship to wait for the Queen.

"I was right about him," Obi-Wan said softly, eyeing the boy. "I mean no disrespect, Master, but it is the truth."

"From *your* point of view," Qui-Gon replied.

"The boy is dangerous," Obi-Wan insisted. "They all sense it. Why can't you?"

"His fate is uncertain, not dangerous," Qui-Gon replied. "The Council will decide Anakin's future. That should be enough for you. Now get on board!"

Obi-Wan reluctantly climbed aboard the vessel, followed by R2-D2. Qui-Gon watched until they were inside, then walked toward Anakin.

The boy glanced at him uncomfortably. "Master Qui-Gon, sir, I don't want to be a problem."

This dangerous child was on the verge of tears. How could they label him this way—because he felt the pain of first separation from his mother? Because he showed a bit of frustration?

"You won't be a problem, Annie." Qui-Gon knelt to

face him eye-to-eye. "I'm not allowed to train you, so I want you to watch me and be mindful. Always remember, your focus determines your reality. Stay close to me and you will be safe."

"Master, sir, I've been wondering—what are midi-chlorians?"

"Midi-chlorians are a microscopic life-form that resides within all living cells and communicates with the Force."

The boy's eyes grew large. "They live inside of me?"

Qui-Gon nodded. "In your cells. We are symbionts with the midi-chlorians."

"Symbionts?"

"Life-forms living together for mutual advantage. Without the midi-chlorians, life could not exist, and we would have no knowledge of the Force. They continually speak to you, telling you the will of the Force."

"They *do*?"

"When you learn to quiet your mind, you will hear them speak to you."

Anakin cocked his head curiously. "I don't understand."

"With time and training, Annie," Qui-Gon said with a reassuring smile, "you will."

Two air taxis now emerged from the Senate building and *whooshed* onto the landing platform. Captain Panaka climbed out of the first vehicle, followed by a small squadron of officers and guards. From the other taxi stepped Queen Amidala, her handmaidens, and Jar Jar.

Qui-Gon approached the Queen and bowed. "Your Highness, it is our pleasure to continue to serve and protect you."

"I welcome your help," Queen Amidala replied. "Senator Palpatine fears the Trade Federation means to destroy me."

"I promise you I will not let that happen."

The Queen nodded gratefully and boarded the ship.

Jar Jar leaped across the floor and threw his arms around Qui-Gon. "WESA GOEN HOME!"

* * *

As the ship sped away from Coruscant, the Queen told Qui-Gon the sad news: The Senate hadn't passed the resolution, and so she was heading home to a planet under siege.

"After my plea," the Queen reported, "the Supreme Chancellor tried forcefully to decree a condemnation against the Trade Federation's actions in Naboo."

"Valorum is a good man," Qui-Gon remarked.

"Yes, but not a strong one. He was immediately approached by various meddlesome bureaucrats who reminded him that the decree was against procedure. So Valorum withdrew the motion and asked that a *committee* be appointed to investigate."

"A committee? By the time they would finish—"

"Exactly. It was unacceptable. The level of my frustration was matched only by that of Senator Palpatine, who suggested I move for a vote of no confidence in Chancellor Valorum. The motion was carried, and Valorum stepped down."

Qui-Gon was amazed. This was an extraordinary move. The Queen carried an air of stillness and ceremony, but her actions cut like blaster fire. "Who will take his place?"

"One of the nominees," the Queen replied, "is Senator Palpatine."

Palpatine. His election might break the deadlock. It would certainly be a boon for Naboo.

Queen Amidala gazed over Qui-Gon's shoulder. "Your young charge seems to have regained his spirit."

Qui-Gon turned. Anakin was standing behind Ric Olié, grilling him about the cockpit controls. "And...*that* one?" he asked.

"The forward stabilizer," Olié replied.

"And *those* control the pitch?"

Olié chuckled. "You catch on pretty quick."

"Come," Queen Amidala said, turning toward her chamber. "It is time for our strategy meeting with Captain Panaka."

Qui-Gon escorted her into the room. Two of the

Queen's handmaidens, Eirtaé and Sabé, were waiting, along with Panaka, Obi-Wan, and Jar Jar.

The captain spoke with great urgency. "Your Highness, the moment we land, the Trade Federation will arrest you and force you to sign the treaty."

"I agree," Qui-Gon said. "I'm not sure what you hope to accomplish by this."

"I'm going to take back what is ours," the Queen said resolutely.

"There are only twelve of us, Your Highness," Captain Panaka pointed out. "We have no army."

"I cannot fight a war for you, Your Highness," Qui-Gon added, "only protect you."

The Queen met his glance levelly, fearlessly. She said nothing for a long time, gazing slowly around the room.

She was young and energetic—but also smart, Qui-Gon knew. She would, in the end, take only the most prudent measures.

"Jar Jar Binks!" the Queen suddenly called out.

Jar Jar nearly jumped. "*Mesa*, Your Highness?"

"Yes," Amidala said firmly. "I need your help."

CHAPTER FOUR

The Queen's plan was a huge risk.

Involving the Gungans? It would be a risky move.

Qui-Gon fought the urge to judge. It was not his place. His job was to support and protect Amidala in whatever she decided for her people.

The Naboo citizens were prisoners now. And desperate circumstances required desperate measures.

From a distance, the green lushness of Naboo's landscape gave no hint of an embattled, defeated civilization. Even the cluster of Trade Federation ships that had surrounded the planet was nowhere in evidence.

"I have one battleship on my scope," Ric Olié announced.

"A droid control ship," Obi-Wan said.

"They've probably spotted us," Panaka guessed.

Obi-Wan nodded. "We haven't much time."

The cabin fell silent as Olié skillfully navigated around the battleship's field of detection. He swept around to the opposite side of the planet, on the Queen's strict orders to land near the swamp that contained Otoh Gunga.

The touchdown was peaceful and apparently unnoticed. While Jar Jar left to summon the Gungans to the Queen, Qui-Gon and Obi-Wan waited.

The Padawan seemed particularly quiet and uneasy. "Do you think the Queen's idea will work?" he finally asked.

"The Gungans will not be easily swayed,"

Qui-Gon replied, "and we cannot use our power to help her."

"I'm...I'm sorry for my behavior, Master," Obi-Wan said. "It is not my place to disagree with you about the boy. I am grateful you think I am ready for the trials."

"You have been a good apprentice. You are much wiser than I am, Obi-Wan. I foresee you will become a great Jedi Knight."

Obi-Wan smiled. Qui-Gon put his arm around the young man's shoulder and walked to the edge of the swamp, where the others were waiting—the Queen, her three handmaidens, Captain Panaka, Anakin, four pilots, eight guards, and R2-D2.

It seemed hours before Jar Jar finally emerged. But his rubbery face was glum. "Daresa nobody dare! All gone. Some kinda fight, mesa tinks."

"Do you think they have been taken to camps?" Captain Panaka asked.

"More likely they were wiped out," Obi-Wan guessed.

Jar Jar shook his head. "Mesa no tink so. When in trouble, Gungans go to sacred place. Come on, mesa show you."

Jar Jar turned, walking briskly into the swampy jungle.

They all followed, trudging for miles. Jar Jar took turns where no paths existed, never breaking stride, moving in a tortuous route that seemed to cross over itself a hundred times.

Finally he stopped, in an area that looked no different than any other they had passed through. He began to sniff the air. "Dissen it," he said with a confident nod.

He threw back his head let out a strange chattering noise.

From deep in the woods, seven Gungan troops emerged. They carried electropoles and rode on native four-legged kaadus. Leading them was Captain Tarpals, who had taken Jar Jar prisoner during Qui-Gon's visit to Otoh Gunga.

"Heyo-dalee, Captain Tarpals!" Jar Jar exclaimed.

Tarpals looked disgusted. "Binks—noah gain!"

"Wesa comen to see da boss."

"Ouch time, Binks," Tarpals said, shaking his head. "Ouch time for all-n youse."

He turned his kaadu back into the forest and gestured for the others to follow.

Before long, they reached a clearing where hundreds of Gungans stood among the ruins of a great temple. Enormous carved heads lay toppled on the wet, marshy ground, their eyes staring at the intruders.

From behind one of the heads emerged a massive Gungan, wearing a robe and an angry scowl—Boss Nass.

Jar Jar flinched.

"Jar Jar Binks!" the Boss thundered. "Who's da uss-en others?"

Queen Amidala stepped forward. "I am Queen Amidala of Naboo. I come before you in peace."

"Naboo biggen." Boss Nass glared at her. "Yousa bringen da Mackineeks. Yousa all bombad. Yousa all die-n, mesa tink."

At once, the Gungan troops pointed their power poles toward the Queen, but she stood fast, saying only, "We wish to form an alliance."

Suddenly, one of her handmaidens stepped forward to speak. This, too, was part of the plan. On Tatooine, Padmé Naberrie had demonstrated bravery and cunning. Now, she would need both.

"Your honor—" she began.

"Whosa *dis*?" Boss Nass demanded.

"*I* am Queen Amidala."

The Boss stiffened with surprise. The Gungans fell into a stunned silence. Anakin's jaw fell open.

Padmé—the real Queen—gestured toward the handmaiden who was dressed as Amidala. "This is my decoy—my protection, my loyal bodyguard. I am sorry for my deception, but under the circumstances it has become necessary to protect myself. Although we do not always agree, Your Honor, our two great societies have always lived in peace—until now. The Trade Federation has destroyed all that we have worked so hard to build. You are in hiding—my people are in camps. If we do not act quickly, all will be lost forever. I ask you to help us—no, I *beg* you to help us."

As the Naboo people watched in shock, Queen Amidala slowly fell to her knees. "We are your humble servants. Our fate is in your hands."

Captain Panaka strode forward. He too knelt before the Boss.

One by one, his troops joined him.

And Queen Amidala's handmaidens.

And Anakin.

And finally, Qui-Gon, Obi-Wan, and Jar Jar.

Boss Nass chuckled. "Yousa no tinken yousa greater den da Gungans! Mesa like dis. Maybe wesa bein friends!"

At this point, you must decide whether to continue reading this adventure, or to play your own adventure in the Star Wars Adventures *The Final Battle* Game Book.

To play your own adventure, turn to the first page of the Game Book and follow the directions you find there.

To continue reading this adventure, turn the page!

CHAPTER FIVE

Captain Panaka had been gone for hours to see if he could find any fugitive Naboo citizens hiding in the jungles. Queen Amidala had been discussing battle plans with the five Gungan generals for hours as well.

The Queen was young, the Gungans were fearless—but none had been tested in battle. Their words were brave and smart, but also reckless.

Qui-Gon and Obi-Wan stayed quiet. Becoming involved in the affairs of Naboo was a breach of the Jedi covenant. They could only discharge their duties—protecting the Queen—and nothing else.

Of course, if she *asked* their opinion, they were obliged to give it. So they never strayed far from her side.

Suddenly a lookout shouted, "Daza comin!"

"All right!" Anakin whooped. "They're here!"

The Gungans murmured with excitement. Boss Nass was puffed up with the idea of war. He smiled at Jar Jar and put his arm solemnly around the smaller Gungan's shoulder. "Yousa doen grand! Jar Jar bringen da Naboo together."

"Oh, no, no, no, no..." Jar Jar said modestly.

"So," the Boss continued, "wesa maken yousa Bombad General."

"*GENERAL?*" Jar Jar stiffened. His eyes rolled back and he flopped onto the ground in dead faint.

Qui-Gon heard the *whoosh* of approaching speeders—*Naboo* speeders.

Panaka was the first to come to a stop in the clearing. He was followed by his own troops—and some new ones, all Naboo citizens. As they exited the speeders, Panaka quickly dismounted and ran to the group.

"What is the situation?" the Queen asked.

"Almost everyone's in camps," Panaka replied. "A few hundred police and guards have formed an underground movement. I brought as many of the leaders as I could. The Trade Federation Army's also much larger than we thought—and much stronger. Your Highness, this is a battle I do not think we can win."

"The battle is a diversion," the Queen asserted. "The Gungans must draw the droid army away from the cities. We can enter the city using the secret passages on the waterfall side. Once we get to the main entrance, Captain Panaka will create a diversion so that we can enter the palace and capture the viceroy. Without the viceroy, they will be lost and confused. What do you think, Master Jedi?"

"The viceroy will be well guarded," Qui-Gon remarked.

Captain Panaka nodded. "The difficulty's getting into the throne room. Once we're inside, we shouldn't have a problem."

"There is a possibility with this diversion many Gungans will be killed," Qui-Gon warned.

"Wesa ready to do oursa part!" Boss Nass declared.

"We have a plan that should immobilize the droid army," the Queen said. "We will send what pilots we have to knock out the Droid Control Ship that is orbiting the planet. If we can get past their shields, we can sever communications, and their droids will be helpless."

"A well conceived plan," Qui-Gon said. "However, there's great risk. The weapons on your fighters may not penetrate the shields."

"And there's an even bigger danger," Obi-Wan spoke up. "If the viceroy escapes, Your Highness, he will return with another droid army."

"That is why we must not fail to get the viceroy," the Queen replied matter-of-factly. "Everything depends on it."

CHAPTER SIX

The plaza was crawling with droids and tanks.

Qui-Gon pulled his head back behind the marble wall, where Obi-Wan and Queen Amidala stood tensely with Anakin, R2-D2, the handmaiden named Eirtaé, and about twenty Naboo guards.

The hangar door was close, maybe twenty yards away. Across the plaza, similarly hidden, were Captain Panaka and his team.

Queen Amidala took out a small laser device and signaled Panaka.

Qui-Gon leaned down to Anakin. "Once we get inside, Annie, you find a safe place to hide, and stay there."

"Sure," Anakin replied.

"And *stay there*," Qui-Gon repeated pointedly.

DZZZZZZT! DZZZZZZZZT!

Blaster fire rang out. The droids instantly turned their backs, rushing toward the other side of the plaza.

The diversion cleared the plaza. Queen Amidala and her team raced across it and through the hangar door.

Inside, the droid force was smaller—but not nearly as small as Qui-Gon had hoped.

DZZZZZZZZT!

A blast screamed toward the Queen. Qui-Gon reached with his lightsaber and blocked it. The beam reversed back to the shooter, a droid who vaporized into a cloud of black smoke.

The team ran for cover. Blaster fire crisscrossed overhead, zinging off the hangar walls.

The Queen drew her blaster and returned fire. Qui-Gon and Obi-Wan stood by her, deflecting shots until her troops found cover. Anakin peeled off from the rest and hid behind one of the Naboo fighter ships.

As the Queen's troops opened fire, the sound of exploding droids rang through the hangar.

"Get to your ships!" she shouted.

Behind her, the Naboo pilots raced for the fighter ships.

As they settled inside, one by one the ships levitated and took off. Out of the corner of his eye, Qui-Gon spotted Anakin hiding in the cockpit of an unused ship.

Good. The droids wouldn't be firing there.

BOOOOOM!

Qui-Gon flinched. Outside, a Naboo Starfighter burst into flames, shot by a Trade Federation tank.

But the other ships had broken away and were soaring into the sky.

Captain Panaka's troops stormed into the hangar door. The droid defense had been disabled.

Inside, they helped blast the few remaining droids into scrap metal.

In the smoky, metallic silence, the Queen called out, "My guess is the viceroy is in the throne room!"

The teams hurried across the hangar. As they

neared the exit, Anakin's head popped up from inside one the star fighters. "Hey, wait for me!" he called.

"No, Annie, you stay there," Qui-Gon commanded. "Stay right where you are."

"But I—"

"*Stay in that cockpit!*"

As the team reached the door, they suddenly stopped, falling back into defensive positions.

Qui-Gon grabbed his lightsaber, preparing for another assault.

But no droid army was entering, no battalion of warriors. Only one man blocked the door.

And he was more than enough.

On the Tatooine desert the warrior had been a predatory blur, but now Qui-Gon had a clear look. The face was hideous, tattooed in a jagged death-mask pattern of red and black. A ring of horns surrounded his head, and his yellow, soulless eyes glared only at Qui-Gon.

A Jedi felt no fear. That was part of the training, the creed. As a Jedi, Qui-Gon had long ago put aside fear in the service of his duty.

But as a human, he knew no feeling was ever truly forgotten.

The Sith Lord raised a lightsaber.

CHAPTER SEVEN

The Queen and Captain Panaka looked uncertainly at the two Jedi.

"We'll handle this," Qui-Gon murmured.

The Sith Lord snapped his wrists, holding his weapon sideways. Two columns of light shot out, left and right.

A double lightsaber. Twice as deadly.

Qui-Gon and Obi-Wan drew their weapons.

The Sith Lord lunged. Qui-Gon blocked one thrust, which nearly knocked him off his feet.

Obi-Wan struck hard, but the Sith Lord's reflexes were astonishing. He blocked the thrust and sent Obi-Wan flying.

The Jedi sprang to their feet and swung at him from either side. But the Sith Lord moved as if defying the laws of physics, deflecting and attacking them both.

Soon, he was not alone. Through the hangar door rolled three enormous metal wheels that unfolded to become destroyer droids.

They skittered forward, firing on the Naboo troops. Qui-Gon did not notice them. He could not take his eyes from the Sith Lord.

A sudden explosion rocked the hangar. Three destroyer droids blasted apart, attacked by—

Anakin's starfighter!

The boy had taken the controls, and the vehicle rolled down the runway, picking off the destroyers one by one.

The Sith Lord swung hard and Qui-Gon nearly got it in the head. He could not afford to worry about the boy.

As the Naboo troops escaped through the hangar door, the two Jedi stepped up their assault on the Sith Lord. But he was like a mirror, taking their energy and reflecting it back magnified.

He drove Qui-Gon and Obi-Wan forward through the hangar. They backed into a doorway that swung open, leading onto a narrow catwalk.

They were in the heart of the Theed power generator now, a cavernous pit crisscrossed by beams and walkways around the planet's main generator. Below them the bottom dropped into a black void.

Downthrust. Uppercut. Sideswipe. The Sith Lord whirled as if the catwalk held no danger.

As he turned toward Obi-Wan, Qui-Gon lunged. He brought his lightsaber down hard toward the Sith Lord's shoulder.

The evil warrior spun. With a deft block, he deflected the blow, then followed through with a kick to Obi-Wan's arm. The Padawan's lightsaber went flying over the edge of the catwalk.

And so did Obi-Wan.

He fell fast, unfolding his body gracefully and reaching out. His fingers grabbed onto the edge of a catwalk, several levels down. He held tight, hanging for his life.

Qui-Gon let loose a kick that sent the Sith Lord

flying. His fall was broken by a catwalk two levels below.

Qui-Gon leaped after him. But the Sith Lord jumped to his feet and ran.

Just below them, Obi-Wan climbed to safety. Summoning the Force, he sprang upward, high above his own level, and landed on the catwalk behind Qui-Gon.

The Sith Lord raced through a small door and into a long hallway. Qui-Gon was close behind him, and Obi-Wan took pursuit.

With a sudden sharp hum, solid vertical walls of energy appeared, blocking the hallway. Qui-Gon stopped short, inches away from being vaporized.

On the other side of the energy wall, the Sith Lord mocked Qui-Gon with taunting facial expressions.

Nothing could happen now until the walls parted.

Be in the moment, Qui-Gon told himself.

The Sith Lord had shaken him. He would need to regain his balance.

Qui-Gon sat. Closing his eyes, he meditated and waited.

When the hum stopped and the wall disappeared, he charged.

The Sith Lord was at the end of the corridor now. It had become a walkway again, suspended over a new chamber, a deep melting pit.

Nothing existed below them now. Nothing but blackness.

The energy walls had appeared again. Obi-Wan was trapped behind the last one, separated from Qui-Gon by the thickness of a subatomic particle.

Qui-Gon went after the Sith Lord with all he had— a fury of lightsaber slashes that sent the black-clad warrior reeling.

The Sith Lord struck back with his blades, but neither came close.

So he hit Qui-Gon on the jaw.

As the Jedi Master's head snapped back, he felt a sudden, sharp pain. It started in his abdomen and quickly spread through his legs and arms.

The Sith Lord had stopped moving. His wrist was wrapped around the hilt of his lightsaber.

The blade was deep in Qui-Gon's body.

Coolly, the Sith Lord pulled it out. Qui-Gon gasped, falling to his knees in a white shock of silence. He heard a scream, but it was not his own. Through the haze of his ebbing eyesight, he saw the wall of electrons part and his Padawan rush forward. He saw the crossing of blades and the tumult of moving bodies.

And then, finally, he saw a mighty swing that passed through the Sith Lord. And he saw a black shape fall silently over the edge and into the pit.

Obi-Wan had killed a Dark Lord.

Qui-Gon smiled weakly.

He had been right. The young man was indeed ready.

"*Master!*" Obi-Wan's wail was unlike anything Qui-Gon had ever heard from him. He knelt by Qui-Gon and cradled him. "*MASTER!*"

"It is too late," Qui-Gon said. "It's—"

"NO!"

"Obi-Wan, promise..." The words hurt. They seared his insides. "...promise me you'll train the boy..."

"Yes, Master—"

"He is the Chosen One." Qui-Gon had to get the words out. Obi-Wan was the only hope now. The only one the boy trusted. "The boy will...bring balance.... Train...him!"

The last thing Qui-Gon heard, before his eyes shut forever, was the sound of his Padawan weeping.

At this point, readers who chose to follow the adventure in the Star Wars Adventures Game Book can return to the novel *The Final Battle*.

EPILOGUE

The Starfighters had failed.

The Gungan defense had been stopped by the relentless droid hordes.

But the boy had turned it around.

The boy had penetrated to the interior of the Trade Federation battleship and blown up the main reactor. Section by section, the entire vehicle had exploded into a nova of space debris.

Without power, the droids had gone limp. The Queen and Captain Panaka, having sneaked into the chamber of the viceroy, were able to secure a total surrender.

And Senator Palpatine had been elected Supreme Chancellor.

It had all happened so fast.

And it wouldn't have happened without Anakin.

The Chosen One.

Was it true? Perhaps.

Obi-Wan wanted to believe his Master's judgment. But even now, even after Anakin's feats, Obi-Wan couldn't totally shake his doubts about the boy.

Nevertheless, he had made a promise to Qui-Gon. And he would follow through. He would train the boy to be a Jedi.

Assuming that he himself became a Knight. That was still to be determined.

Obi-Wan swallowed hard and entered the turret

room of the Theed palace. There Yoda awaited, pacing slowly.

Kneeling, Obi-Wan faced the aged Master.

Yoda's face was unrevealing. He continued to pace, as if oblivious to the young man. Then, finally, he spoke: "Confer on you, the level of Jedi Knight the Council does. But agree with your taking this boy as your Padawan learner, I do not."

"Qui-Gon believed in him," Obi-Wan protested. "I believe in Qui-Gon."

Yoda shook his head. "The Chosen One the boy may be. Nevertheless, grave danger I fear in his training."

"Master Yoda, I gave Qui-Gon my word. I *will* train Anakin—without the approval of the Council, if I must."

"Qui-Gon's defiance I sense in you—need that, you do not," Yoda said, looking sharply at Obi-Wan. He paused, his expression softening. "Agree with you, the Council does. Your apprentice, young Skywalker will be."

Obi-Wan beamed. He was not only a Jedi. He had a mission.

He wanted to jump up and twirl the grizzled old warrior in the air. But he saw Qui-Gon's face in his mind's eye—and he heard his Master's words.

Stay in the moment.

He checked his emotions and solemnly bowed.

And he thought he saw a hint of a smile on Yoda's wrinkled face.

* * *

The funeral pyre, as per tradition, occurred that night.

Qui-Gon's body burned slowly, as if the spirit had lingered on and was putting up a last fight. But the figure in the funeral pyre was no longer a man. It was a reminder.

Obi-Wan stared at the silhouette until it was consumed—until the contours of the heroic face burned into his heart and mind, the places where Qui-Gon's soul would always live, and always advise.

Behind Obi-Wan, a drum rolled steadily and then faded. Someone released doves, which flew into the rising ashes and disappeared on the wind.

Next to Obi-Wan stood the boy, his eyes red and fearful. "He is one with the Force, Anakin," Obi-Wan said. "You must let go."

"What will happen to me now?" the boy asked.

"I am your Master now," Obi-Wan reassured him. "You will become a Jedi, I promise."

On Obi-Wan's other side, Mace Windu turned to Yoda. "There is no doubt," the Jedi Councilman said, "the mysterious warrior was a Sith."

Yoda nodded. "Always two, there are—no more, no less. A Master and an apprentice."

"But which one was destroyed?" Mace Windu asked. "The Master or the apprentice?"

Obi-Wan stood close to his new young Padawan. If he was indeed the Chosen One, his training must be swift.

He would be needed for a new battle, one far greater than anything yet faced.

And he had better be ready.